The Boxcar Children Mysteries

THE GUIDE DOG MYSTERY
THE HURRICANE MYSTERY
THE PET SHOP MYSTERY
THE MYSTERY OF THE SECRET
  MESSAGE
THE FIREHOUSE MYSTERY
THE MYSTERY IN SAN
  FRANCISCO
THE NIAGARA FALLS MYSTERY
THE MYSTERY AT THE ALAMO
THE OUTER SPACE MYSTERY
THE SOCCER MYSTERY
THE MYSTERY IN THE OLD
  ATTIC
THE GROWLING BEAR
  MYSTERY
THE MYSTERY OF THE LAKE
  MONSTER
THE MYSTERY AT PEACOCK
  HALL
THE WINDY CITY MYSTERY
THE BLACK PEARL MYSTERY
THE CEREAL BOX MYSTERY
THE PANTHER MYSTERY
THE MYSTERY OF THE
  QUEEN'S JEWELS
THE STOLEN SWORD MYSTERY
THE BASKETBALL MYSTERY
THE MOVIE STAR MYSTERY
THE MYSTERY OF THE PIRATE'S
  MAP
THE GHOST TOWN MYSTERY
THE MYSTERY OF THE BLACK
  RAVEN
THE MYSTERY IN THE MALL
THE MYSTERY IN NEW YORK
THE GYMNASTICS MYSTERY
THE POISON FROG MYSTERY
THE MYSTERY OF THE EMPTY
  SAFE
THE HOME RUN MYSTERY
THE GREAT BICYCLE RACE
  MYSTERY

THE MYSTERY OF THE WILD
  PONIES
THE MYSTERY IN THE
  COMPUTER GAME
THE MYSTERY AT THE
  CROOKED HOUSE
THE HOCKEY MYSTERY
THE MYSTERY OF THE
  MIDNIGHT DOG
THE MYSTERY OF THE
  SCREECH OWL
THE SUMMER CAMP MYSTERY
THE COPYCAT MYSTERY
THE HAUNTED CLOCK TOWER
  MYSTERY
THE MYSTERY OF THE TIGER'S
  EYE
THE DISAPPEARING STAIRCASE
  MYSTERY
THE MYSTERY ON BLIZZARD
  MOUNTAIN
THE MYSTERY OF THE SPIDER'S
  CLUE
THE CANDY FACTORY MYSTERY
THE MYSTERY OF THE
  MUMMY'S CURSE
THE MYSTERY OF THE STAR
  RUBY
THE STUFFED BEAR MYSTERY
THE MYSTERY OF ALLIGATOR
  SWAMP
THE MYSTERY AT SKELETON
  POINT
THE TATTLETALE MYSTERY
THE COMIC BOOK MYSTERY
THE GREAT SHARK MYSTERY
THE ICE CREAM MYSTERY
THE MIDNIGHT MYSTERY
THE MYSTERY IN THE
  FORTUNE COOKIE
THE BLACK WIDOW SPIDER
  MYSTERY
THE RADIO MYSTERY

THE RADIO MYSTERY

created by
GERTRUDE CHANDLER WARNER

Illustrated by Hodges Soileau

SCHOLASTIC INC.
New York Toronto London Auckland Sydney
New Delhi Mexico City Hong Kong Buenos Aires

ISBN 0-439-51750-8

12 11 10 9 8 7 6 5 4 3 2 1   3 4 5 6 7 8/0

Printed in the U.S.A.   40
First Scholastic printing, November 2003

Contents

CHAPTER 1

"Let's Go!"

Rain hammered the roof of the boxcar. Six-year-old Benny Alden looked out the window.

"It's been raining forever," he said with a sigh. Usually he liked playing in the boxcar with his brother and sisters. The four of them had found the boxcar in the woods and lived there for a while, after their parents died. Then their grandfather, James Alden, found them and brought them to live with him in his big white house in Greenfield. Grandfather had the boxcar

towed to his backyard as a special surprise for his grandchildren. When they weren't traveling and having adventures, the Alden children used the boxcar as a playhouse.

"It's only been raining for two days — it just *seems* like forever," twelve-year-old Jessie said, smiling at her younger brother. "Why don't you work on this puzzle with Henry and me?"

"Or paint with me?" ten-year-old Violet offered. "It's a perfect day for using watercolors."

Henry Alden stood up and looked out the window. At fourteen, he was the oldest of the four Alden children. "Here comes Grandfather. He looks like he has news."

Grandfather came into the boxcar shaking his dripping umbrella. "This weather is only good for ducks," he remarked. "But it's nice and dry in here.

"How would you like to go to Pennsylvania for a few days?" Grandfather asked the children.

"Is it about a new mystery?" asked Violet. The Alden children loved solving mysteries.

"How did you guess?" Grandfather replied.

Benny didn't need to hear any more. "Let's go!"

Jessie laughed. "Benny's always in a hurry to go solve a new mystery."

"What's the mystery about?" Henry asked.

"I'll tell you everything once we're on the road," said Grandfather. "I'd like to be in Pennsylvania before dinner."

An hour later, the Aldens left Connecticut behind and were on their way to Deer Crossing, Pennsylvania.

"So why are we going to Deer Crossing?" Henry asked.

Grandfather changed lanes, then replied, "This morning I got a call from my friend Jocelyn Hawley. She lives in Deer Crossing and runs a local radio station. Jocelyn didn't want to go into detail over the phone, but apparently the station is in some kind of trouble. I've told her before what great detectives my grandchildren are, and she asked if you would come and help."

"Wow!" said Benny. "Do you think we'll get to see inside the station?"

"I'm sure of it," Grandfather said.

As they crossed the Pennsylvania border, the rain cleared and the sun broke through the clouds. After a while, Grandfather turned off the interstate and onto a road along Deer River. A tall metal tower with a blinking red light and the letters WCXZ loomed over the village of Deer Crossing.

"That tower must be part of the radio station," said Henry. He checked the directions Grandfather had given him. "Jocelyn Hawley's house should be at the end of this street."

"It's been a while since I was last here," Grandfather said.

A large redbrick house with a wide, welcoming front porch stood on a hill before them. As the Aldens' minivan climbed the gravel driveway, two figures came out of the house.

A woman about Grandfather's age smiled

warmly and waved as they stepped out of the car. "I'm so glad you came," said Jocelyn Hawley. She wore slacks and a blue sweater that brought out the blue in her eyes. Dangly silver earrings set off her short gray hair.

"I'm overdue for a visit," Grandfather said. "Let me introduce my grandchildren, Henry, Jessie, Violet, and Benny. Children, meet Jocelyn Hawley."

"You guys are the detectives?" said the girl standing beside Jocelyn. She was about Henry's age, tall and slim, with long red hair.

"And very good ones, from what I hear," Jocelyn said. "This is my granddaughter, Gwen."

"Hi," Gwen said. She smiled, but not as warmly as Jocelyn.

Jocelyn moved toward the front door. "Let's go inside so you can get settled. Dinner is nearly ready. We can talk while we eat."

The Aldens were given the top floor of the Hawley house. When they had unpacked, the children and Grandfather trooped downstairs to the large family room, where snacks had been set out in front of a low, snapping fire.

"Help yourself," Gwen said, pointing to glasses and a pitcher of cranberry juice on the coffee table. After they had finished their snacks, the Aldens helped Gwen carry everything back to the kitchen. Then Jocelyn called them to supper.

When everyone's plate was loaded with spaghetti, green salad, and warm bread, Jocelyn began her story.

"My husband, Luther, bought the radio station many years ago, just after we were married," she told the Aldens. "It was a lovely station with programs like a household hints show, a breakfast show, easy-listening music, and live dramas."

"I've always tuned into the station on business trips," said Grandfather. "Luther was a great DJ."

"Luther called the station the heartbeat of Deer Crossing," said Jocelyn. "He never made much money because he did things the old-fashioned way. But he loved that station."

The Aldens smiled and Jocelyn went on. "Once a man from a big corporation offered Luther a lot of money to sell the station. The man wanted to cancel Luther's old-fashioned radio shows and play 'all hits, all the time.' "

"What happened?" asked Henry.

Gwen passed the breadbasket. "Gramp refused," she said proudly. "He said no amount of money would make him give up his old programs."

"The man left," Jocelyn added. "He knew Luther would never change his mind."

Grandfather smiled. "Luther always knew exactly what he wanted."

Jocelyn smiled back. "After Luther died, people asked me if I'd change the format to something more modern."

"Like 'all hits, all the time?' " Violet guessed.

Jocelyn nodded. "But I didn't. The radio station really *is* the heartbeat of Deer

Crossing. And I love the old-fashioned programs just as much as Luther did. I'm proud of the station and of the programs we play."

"I like it, too," Gwen put in. "Gran's station is really fun to listen to. It's the kind of radio people had back in the old days, before everyone had a television. We even put on a live mystery show. I'm the sound engineer," she added proudly.

"A live mystery show!" Benny repeated. "That sounds great!"

"The episodes are twenty minutes a day, five days a week," Jocelyn told them. "Each week we do a new play. A local woman writes the scripts and waiters and waitresses from the Route 11 Diner act for free. And Gwen does the sound effects. She's very good."

"Sounds like fun," Henry said.

"It *was* fun," Jocelyn said sadly. "Until these things started happening."

"What kinds of things?" Jessie wanted to know.

"Lights going out, blood-curdling screams," Gwen replied with a shiver. "People think it's a ghost."

"That's just a story," Jocelyn said.

Benny's eyes grew big. "Why would a ghost haunt a radio station?"

"Not just any ghost," said Gwen mysteriously. "We have our very own *special* ghost at station WCXZ."

CHAPTER 2

The Ghost of Station WCXZ

"A special ghost!" Benny breathed, awestruck. "Tell us about it!"

"Let's have dessert first," Jocelyn said.

Everyone helped clear the table while Gwen brought in dishes of chocolate pudding with whipped cream.

"Years ago," Jocelyn said, "radio stations put on plays. Writers wrote the plays, and actors read the parts on the air. The radio plays were very popular. The actors whose shows were on the air in big cities were sometimes very famous."

"Like people on TV these days," Jessie said.

Jocelyn nodded. "Many, many years ago, there was a young woman in Deer Crossing who wanted to be a radio star. Her name was Daphne Owens. She played in nearly every radio show on WCXZ. Those shows could only be heard in Deer Crossing, but Daphne was sure her big break was just around the corner."

"Big break?" Violet asked.

"Onto a show at a bigger radio station," Gwen explained. "If she got on one of the city stations, millions of people would hear her."

Jocelyn went on. "One day, Daphne heard about a talent scout from the city, who was visiting small stations, looking for good actors to hire. Daphne bragged to everyone in town that when the talent scout heard her, he would hire her on the spot. Soon she'd be famous."

"What happened?" Benny asked.

"The day the talent scout came to WCXZ, a huge thunderstorm disrupted the broadcast," Jocelyn said. "The lights went out and the equipment went haywire. The talent scout didn't have time to wait. He went on to the next station."

"What did Daphne do?" Henry asked.

"Daphne lost her big chance," said Jocelyn. "She didn't show up for work the next day. Or the next."

"She was never seen in town again," Gwen said dramatically.

"People guessed Daphne was so upset, she just picked up and moved," Jocelyn said. "But nobody knew for sure."

"She never called or wrote to anyone in Deer Crossing?" Jessie asked.

Jocelyn shook her head. "Not a word. It was very strange. After a while, people quit worrying about her."

"At the station, they joke that Daphne Owens is 'haunting' the place whenever anything goes wrong," Gwen said.

"It's no joke now," Jocelyn said seriously. "The last few times the lights have gone out, objects have mysteriously disappeared. So far, the station has lost a headset and a set of rare records. These 'hauntings' are costing the station a lot of money."

"People blame the ghost for the stolen things?" Violet wanted to know.

"Not me," Jocelyn said. "I don't believe in ghosts."

"The strange things always seem to happen while we're broadcasting the daily mystery show," Gwen said. "Some of the cast members are threatening to quit. They're scared."

"Can you hire new actors?" Henry wanted to know.

Jocelyn sighed. "That's another problem. The cast works for free. If they quit, I don't know how I'll find anyone else willing to work for nothing. I can't afford to pay them. And I'm worried that if things keep going wrong during the live mystery show, people will stop listening."

Gwen shook her head sadly. "That would be awful."

"That's why I called you," Jocelyn concluded. "I'm hoping you'll be able to help us find the ghost."

"We'd be happy to help," Henry said, speaking for them all.

"That's great," Jocelyn said, relieved. "Gwen will take you to the station tomorrow morning. You can watch the live mystery broadcast and look for clues."

As the Aldens headed upstairs to their rooms, Gwen stopped them.

"My grandmother really loves that station," she said. "I hope you know what you're doing."

Jessie looked at her, surprised. "We'll do our best."

"Your best had better be good enough!" Gwen spun on one heel and left, her long red hair swinging behind her.

"I don't think Gwen likes us," Violet said.

"She's probably just upset about the trouble at the station," Henry said. "We've got a 'ghost' to catch tomorrow. We'd better get to bed."

The next morning, Gwen greeted the Alden children with glasses of fresh orange juice. "Good morning," she said, with no

trace of the night before's unpleasantness.

Grandfather was finishing his breakfast. "If I eat another waffle, I won't be able to move!"

"Great," said Benny. "That leaves more for me."

When they had eaten, the four Aldens and Gwen stacked their dishes in the sink. "The station is right in town," Gwen told them. "It's a short walk."

She led the way down Main Street. They passed the Route 11 Diner, which was across from a small park with a fountain and jogging paths. Next was Earl's Auto Sales, then a small one-story building with WCXZ on the front door.

The kids walked into a tiny lobby facing a glass-walled room. A slender, blond man wearing headphones waved at them. Then he punched some buttons, took off his headphones, and came out, smiling. Music played from speakers mounted near the lobby ceiling.

"You must be the Alden kids," he said. "Jocelyn told me you were coming. I'm Avery Drake."

"Avery is the DJ and engineer," Gwen added.

"Ever been in a radio control booth before?" Avery asked. "Come on in."

The Aldens eagerly followed him inside.

"What's that?" Benny asked, pointing to rows of buttons and dials built into a desk. A box of doughnuts sat on top, next to a green plastic sports water bottle.

"That's called a console," Avery said. "These buttons and switches control the sound, music selections, and commercials that you hear on the radio."

"Nice turntable," Henry commented. "Our grandfather has a record player at home."

"We still play records." Avery held up a large plastic disk. "Before cassettes and CDs, people played records on record players. We have a CD changer, too, but Luther kept his turntables. Some of his records are valuable."

"We heard a set of records was stolen," Jessie said.

Avery's face darkened. "I hope you kids

can get to the bottom of this ghost business. Jocelyn Hawley has had a hard time since Luther died."

"Have you ever seen the ghost?" Benny asked.

"I'm not sure," Avery replied, frowning. "The day the records were stolen, I thought I saw someone — or something — slip out the side door. But when I looked outside, no one was there."

"Who could it have been?" Henry asked.

Avery shook his head. "I have no idea. I only caught a glimpse. The culprit hasn't been leaving any clues behind. I'm almost starting to believe that it really *could* be a ghost."

"Are you the only DJ?" Violet asked.

Avery nodded. "The station airs from nine in the morning until eight at night. It's off the air overnight. If I need a break, like now, I put on a long record. I play pre-programmed shows from six to eight in the evening, so I can go to dinner. I usually go running then, too."

Jessie noticed a blue duffel bag in the corner. A cubby with a curtain drawn halfway revealed hangers and a mirror.

"May I talk into your microphone?" Benny asked.

"Benny!" said Violet.

Avery laughed. "Not this time, Benny. But you can listen on the headset while I cue up a commercial." He slipped the earphones on Benny's head and punched a few buttons on the console. Benny heard the song end and a jingle for Earl's Auto Sales warbled through the headphones.

"It's almost time for the live mystery show," Gwen said, glancing at the clock. "I need to check my tapes and props. Why don't you look around the rest of the station yourselves and meet me in the soundstage in a few minutes?"

The soundstage was another glass-walled room that faced one side of Avery's booth.

Two women and a young man were standing in the center of the soundstage, reading aloud from yellow-covered notebooks. A third woman, with spiky black hair, arranged standing microphones in front of the three readers.

Before Gwen went into the soundstage, she said, "That's DeeDee, Gayle, and Sean. They are our actors this week. Workers at the diner take turns being on the show."

"Let's go down here," Jessie suggested, motioning toward a narrow hallway. The hallway divided the soundstage and control booth. At one end was a door marked EXIT.

"This must be the side door that Avery saw the ghost slip out of," Violet said. "I guess it leads outside."

Benny was examining a gray metal box built into the wall next to the door. "What is this?" asked Benny, pointing to the box.

"It's probably a fuse box," Jessie replied. "We have one that looks like that in our basement. It controls the electric lights and the power."

Off the hall, the Aldens found a small room. Plastic chairs were pulled up around a scarred table in the center of the room. A soda machine stood next to a counter that held a tiny microwave.

"This must be the room where people take breaks," Henry guessed.

Jessie peered into a display cabinet oppo-
site the soda machine. "Look at all the tro-
phies and plaques the station got for being
a local sports sponsor."

Violet noticed a framed black-and-white
picture showing two football players and
a cheerleader in old-fashioned uniforms.
Other photos showed groups of people talking into microphones. A pretty girl with a
ponytail was in nearly every picture.

"I wonder if these are people who used
to work at the radio station," she said.

Gwen stuck her head in the room. "We
just finished the run-through," she said.

"What's that?" asked Violet.

"It's when we read through the script
with the sound effects and everything,"
Gwen answered. "A rehearsal. We're about
to broadcast the show. You'd better come
watch, since you're supposed to be detectives. Be ready for anything," she added.

"Gwen acts like we're the enemy," Jessie
whispered to Henry as they left the breakroom. "I'd like to know why."

The spiky-haired woman who had been

setting up microphones frowned when the Aldens came through the soundstage door with Gwen.

"I'm not crazy about extra kids on the set," she said.

Gwen ignored her. "These are the Aldens," she announced to everyone in the room. "They're visiting."

The actors smiled in the Aldens' direction. The spiky-haired woman kept frowning.

"This is Frances St. Clair," said Gwen, introducing the woman. "She writes the mystery show script and the commercials."

"But I don't plan to stick around Deer Crossing forever writing jingles," Frances said.

"Where are you going?" Benny asked.

"Hollywood," she said. "Just as soon as I finish my movie script. It'll be made into a big movie, and I'll be rich and famous."

"Wow!" Benny was impressed.

"But until then, I have to write these silly radio plays." She handed Henry a yellow-covered notebook. "This is today's show. It's the first episode of a story that will run twenty minutes a day for the rest of the week." Frances lowered her voice so the other people in the room wouldn't hear. "I just hope the actors have all studied their lines. Of course, for amateurs, they aren't half bad, especially the new lady over there." She nodded toward an older woman with iron-gray hair and a pink apron.

"That's DeeDee," Gwen told the Aldens. "She just moved to town and started working at the diner and on our show."

"Why is she wearing an apron?" Benny asked. "Is that part of a costume?"

Gwen smiled. "The actors don't wear costumes for radio plays, Benny. Nobody can *see* them, remember? DeeDee probably has on that apron because she came directly from her shift at the diner, or she'll go right to work when this is over."

Frances clapped her hands. "All right, people, the run-through went fine. We're on the air in two minutes. Places, please. Gwen, are you ready?"

Gwen stood behind her own microphone,

which was set back from the actors. A tape recorder and a box were propped on a stool beside her. She smiled. "Ready!"

"Then let's do it," said Frances. She left the soundstage. Just then, Grandfather and Jocelyn entered the station. They stood in the hall with Frances.

The kids heard the fading notes of a commercial. Then Frances counted down and brought down her arm in a signal. In the hall, a red light that said ON AIR flashed on.

The older woman named DeeDee turned to a young brown-haired actress and said, in a British accent, "Muriel, my dear. Would you like a spot of tea?"

The woman playing Muriel opened her mouth to reply.

But before she spoke, the lights went out.

The ON AIR sign glowed like an eerie red eye as a horrible scream filled the station.

CHAPTER 3

Starring — The Alden Kids!

Violet clapped her hands over her ears. The screaming sound was awful! It sounded as if it came from every direction at once and it seemed to go on forever. Worst of all, it was painfully loud.

Sean clicked on a flashlight. The wavering light flashed across the pale, frightened faces of the other actors huddled in the darkened soundstage.

Suddenly the screeching noise stopped. Avery pushed buttons on the console and music came from the speakers. The lights flickered back on.

DeeDee yelled, "The ghost is back!"

The other actors nodded grimly.

Frances rushed into the soundstage. "Thank heavens I got the lights back on. It wasn't a power outage — some joker just turned them off. And then the ghost came."

Henry said, "That was no ghost. It was obviously a tape of someone screaming."

Avery tapped on the window of his booth, pointing toward the clock.

"We need to get back on the air," Frances said. "Everything's all right now. Actors — Gwen — take your places. Let's start again."

"I can't," said Gwen from her corner.

"What's wrong?" Henry asked, twisting around. Like the actors, the Alden children had frozen in their spots when the lights went out.

Gwen's hand passed through the empty air in front of her. "My microphone is gone. Somebody stole it!"

Jocelyn had just stepped into the room.

She put her hand to her forehead. "Not another one!"

The Aldens ran over to Gwen.

"Did you hear anything?" Benny asked.

Gwen shook her head. "Who could hear anything over that racket?"

"Did you see anything when Sean turned on the flashlight?" Jessie said.

Gwen shook her head. "The thief must have slipped in while the lights were off," she said.

"He — or she — was really quick," Henry concluded.

"Ghosts *are* quick," DeeDee said.

Gwen checked the items in her box. "At least none of my props are missing. But this is the second standing mike that's been stolen." She looked up at her grandmother. "What will we do, Gran?"

Jocelyn stood straighter. Her face looked determined. "We covered the delay with some music," she said. "Now we must go on with the show. For today, you can share a microphone with DeeDee."

"You can have the whole thing," said

DeeDee. "I quit. I'm not working in a haunted radio station!"

"All right, we'll recast DeeDee's role," said Frances. "Gayle, could you read both your part and DeeDee's today?"

"I don't think so, Frances," said Gayle. She turned to Jocelyn and smiled apologetically. "I don't want to work at a haunted radio station, either."

"It's not worth the trouble," Sean added. "We do the radio show because it's fun. But it's not fun anymore with everything going wrong. I'm sorry, Jocelyn."

Jocelyn threw up her hands. "Are you *all* quitting?"

"Yes," said DeeDee, speaking for the group. "As long as strange things keep happening in this station, we won't be back."

With that, the entire cast walked out of the soundstage.

Jaunty music poured from the speakers. Avery Drake came in. "Where is everyone going?"

"They quit," said Frances. "Which is what I ought to do, too."

"Earl Biggs of Earl's Auto Sales just called," said Avery. "He's furious. He said he's not paying top advertising dollars for us to play music during the Mystery Theater time slot."

"You'll have to cancel the show," Frances said, turning to Jocelyn. "We can't put on a radio drama without a cast. And you can't afford to hire actors."

Henry said, "If we find the fake ghost, do you think the cast will come back?"

Jocelyn nodded. "I think they will. They really like doing the show. If we can keep the program going somehow until then."

Violet had an idea. She whispered something to her sister and brothers. They nodded.

"What about us?" Violet said.

Jocelyn stared at her. "What do you mean?"

"We'll act in a play," Violet explained. "Frances could write a mystery show with us in it this week."

"Don't be ridiculous," Frances snorted. "You're kids."

"I think it's a good idea," Grandfather said. "You could do a mystery program for kids!"

They all looked at Jocelyn. "Violet, that's a terrific idea, thank you. I'm all for it — it might save the station."

"Well you can get another writer," Frances said. "I only write adult scripts."

"Please? This will be fun," Benny said.

"I'm not writing a kids' program!" Frances insisted.

Jessie and Henry glanced at each other and she knew they were thinking the same thing. Why didn't Frances want to write a kids' show? Was she hoping this would be the end of the station?

"Your contract says you must write five programs a week," Jocelyn reminded Frances firmly. Then she turned to the Aldens. "Looks like you children are going to be radio stars!"

That afternoon, Gwen told the Aldens everything they'd need to know about the live radio show.

"First you read your scripts. Then we do a rehearsal," she explained. "While you're learning your lines, I come up with ideas for sound effects. Then we're ready for the live broadcast."

"What do you do with all this stuff?" Benny asked, looking through Gwen's box. Inside there were spoons, aluminum foil, rocks, paper, wooden blocks, a hammer, and even a pair of men's shoes.

"That's the stuff I use to make sound effects," Gwen replied. "I use tapes for sounds like creaking doors and barking dogs. But a lot of the noises, I make myself, just like they used to on the old radio shows, before they had tape players. It's fun."

"Make one for us," Jessie said.

"Okay. Close your eyes." The Aldens shut their eyes and listened. Gwen picked up a sheet of paper and rattled it around.

Henry opened his eyes. "It sounds like a crackling fire."

"Exactly!" Gwen put down the paper. "My favorite sound effects are the simple ones."

"That's so cool! Show us another one," Benny said.

Gwen thought for a second, then began walking in place. At first her footsteps were heavy. Then they got lighter and lighter.

Benny scratched his head. "A march?"

"Fading footsteps," Gwen said. "Like somebody is walking out of the room."

"What a cool job!" Violet said admiringly.

Gwen smiled shyly. "A lot of the sound effects I learned from my grandfather. He was teaching me to be a DJ, too. He loved this station." Gwen's face looked sad. "It would be too bad if Gran had to give it up or change it."

"We'll catch that ghost," Benny promised.

They all stood quietly for a minute. Then Gwen glanced at her watch. "It's nearly supper time. We'd better go meet Gran and your grandfather at the diner."

"Good idea!" said Benny.

The Aldens followed Gwen down the sta-

tion's narrow hallway. As they passed the control booth, they met Avery getting ready for his dinner break. A pet expert program played from the speakers. Avery had changed into shorts, a T-shirt, and well-worn running shoes. His office shirt and slacks hung in the curtained cubby.

"Are you going to eat at the diner, too?" Benny asked him.

Avery held up his sports duffel. "I'm going running like I do every evening. I'll eat later. See you all tomorrow morning. Don't worry about Frances — she'll write a great script for you."

The Aldens and Gwen said good-bye to Avery, then walked out of the station toward the diner. The Route 11 Diner was just down the block from the radio station.

"Somebody in the station is playing tricks," Henry said as they walked down Main Street.

"But who?" asked Benny. "We were right there when the ghost came, and I didn't see anything."

"Gwen, you've been there before when

the ghost has struck," Violet said. "Have you ever noticed anything strange?"

"I *do* notice things," Gwen snapped. "Just not when the lights go out."

The Aldens exchanged glances. Why was Gwen so touchy?

When the children entered the diner, Grandfather and Jocelyn waved from a large table by the window.

"I was wondering something," Jessie said to Jocelyn. "Avery told us he thought he saw someone go out the side door after the records were stolen. Is that door locked?"

"Not from the inside," Jocelyn replied. "But you need a key to get in from the out-side. The door automatically locks behind you."

"Who has keys?" Henry asked.

"I do," Gwen said. "Avery, Frances, and Gran, of course. And Earl Biggs."

"Who's he?" asked Benny.

"Earl is the owner of Earl's Auto Sales," said Jocelyn. "The car lot is right next door to the station."

"I think we heard his commercial playing on the radio," Violet said.

Jocelyn nodded. "You probably did. He sponsors the live mystery show and some of our other programs, too."

"Didn't you and Luther and Earl go to school together?" Grandfather asked.

Jocelyn smiled. "Yes. We were all good friends. Right before we graduated, Earl asked me to marry him. But I married Luther instead."

Just then, DeeDee walked over with menus. The red ribbon above her name tag matched the red paper place mats.

"Hello, everyone," DeeDee greeted them. Jocelyn introduced her to Grandfather.

"DeeDee, I was surprised you and the others quit the show today," said Grandfather.

"Well," DeeDee said defensively, "we can't work in a place that's haunted."

"You know perfectly well the station is not haunted," Jocelyn said.

"Everybody in town knows the story of Daphne Owens," the waitress said. "If

Daphne's ghost isn't haunting the station, then who is doing those things?"

"Ghosts aren't real," Violet told her. "There has to be a logical explanation."

"And we'll find it," Henry added.

Suddenly businesslike, DeeDee pulled out her pad and pencil and reeled off the daily specials. When she had taken their orders, she left to fetch their drinks.

"Let's go wash our hands," Jessie suggested.

The rest rooms were near the kitchen.

As Violet was coming out of the ladies' room, DeeDee walked toward her hefting a tray of soft drinks and coffee cups.

"You know," DeeDee said, her voice low. "The station really *is* haunted. You can look for logical explanations all you want, but I'm telling you now, it's Daphne Owens's ghost. You and your sister and brothers better watch out!"

Before Violet could respond, DeeDee left to carry the tray to their table.

Violet waited for Jessie to come out of the rest room, then told her about

DeeDee's warning. "Why would she say that?" Violet finished.

"Maybe she just wants to stir things up," Jessie suggested. "Telling ghost stories gives her something to talk about. Maybe she thinks it's funny."

"Maybe." Violet wasn't so sure.

Despite their worries about the trouble at the station, the Aldens, Gwen, and Jocelyn enjoyed their supper.

When it was time to leave, Grandfather drove everyone back to Jocelyn's in the Aldens' minivan.

Jessie, who was sitting by a window, noticed a man jogging on one of the paths in the park. She leaned closer. Was that Avery Drake? Jessie recognized his blue duffel bag.

Strange, Jessie thought. *Why would Avery be running with his bag?*

CHAPTER 4

A Mysterious Phone Call

"Your first day on the radio!" Jocelyn said, setting platters of eggs, sausage, and toast on the table. "Eat hearty!"

"Mmmm!" Benny said, heaping his plate with food.

Jessie nibbled at her eggs. She was so excited, she had hardly slept the night before. Everyone except Gwen was sitting around the breakfast table. Jessie wondered why Gwen was late. This was an important day!

"I want to thank you children for doing

the show this week," Jocelyn said. "If you hadn't volunteered, we would have had to cancel the program. The station would have lost a lot of money — and our listeners would be very disappointed!"

"Doing the show will be fun," Henry said.

"And it gives us a good excuse to hang around the station looking for clues," Violet added.

Jocelyn gave a ring with two keys on it to Henry. "You should have your own keys. The big one is for the front door of the station. The small one goes to this house."

Gwen breezed into the dining room, her red hair streaming down her back. "I bet you guys never had a mystery like this before," she said. "The ghost hasn't left behind a single clue."

"We've had some pretty tough mysteries," Violet said. "But sooner or later, we always find clues."

Sometimes Gwen acts like she doesn't want *us to solve the mystery*, she thought.

"Good luck today. We'll be listening to

your program," Grandfather said as the kids got ready to leave.

"It'll be the best radio show ever!" Benny declared.

The Aldens and Gwen walked the short distance to the station. Inside, Avery waved hello from the control booth.

Frances St. Clair was in the breakroom, working at the table.

"Is that the script?" Gwen asked.

"I wrote half the night," Frances said grumpily, "but it's finished." She passed out yellow-covered copies to Henry, Violet, Jessie, and Gwen.

Henry read the title on the front cover. " 'The Ghost Dog.' Sounds great."

"Since you can't read that well," Frances told Benny, "I've given you the part of the ghost dog."

Benny was delighted. "Oh, boy! Is it a big dog or a little dog?" He yipped like Watch, their dog back home.

"The script says it's a Labrador retriever," Jessie said. "That's a big dog."

"Woof!" Benny deepened his voice.

"It looks like there are lots more sound effects in this play," Gwen said, "so you can also be my assistant."

Everyone read the play silently. The story was about three children who move into a house haunted by the ghost of a dog that had lived there long ago. Violet played the youngest sister. Jessie and Henry played thirteen-year-old twins.

When they had finished reading the script, Frances said, "We'll do a run-through first. You'll read from the scripts during the broadcast, but you'll also be acting."

"What do you mean?" asked Jessie.

"I mean, I want you to read the lines without *sounding* like you're reading them," Frances answered. "Put lots of expression into your voice. Like this." After clearing her throat, she read one of Violet's lines. " 'What was *that*? It sounded like — a dog howling. But there *is* no dog!' "

Frances made her voice high and breathless. She sounded exactly like a scared child.

Henry nodded. "I get it." He found one of his own lines and read it. " 'Look! The dog went right through the wall, just like the wall wasn't there!' " He made his voice sound like he was astonished.

Jessie read one of her lines, too. She enjoyed acting and was very good.

"Now let's hear Benny," Frances said.

Benny practiced howling and barking.

"Good. Practice reading your parts to yourselves for a few minutes and then we'll do the run-through," said Frances.

Then they all headed to the soundstage, where Frances arranged three standing microphones and Gwen set up her box of sound effects props.

Violet felt fluttering in her stomach, like butterflies. She had stage fright! "What if we make a mistake?" she said nervously.

"Mistakes happen. Just keep going," Frances said. "We're broadcasting live, after all. Keep your place in the script and you'll be fine."

Gwen selected the tapes she needed for that day's sound effects. She told Benny,

"I'll do some of the sound effects with props, but mostly I'll use tapes. You can hit the PLAY button on the cassette player when I signal you."

Henry, Jessie, and Violet read through the script, complete with sound effects, with only a few mistakes. Then it was airtime.

Frances counted down the seconds. The red ON AIR sign in the hall flashed on. They were on the radio!

Violet's nervousness vanished as soon as she read her first line. Benny was so good in his part, she almost believed there was an invisible dog.

Henry was surprised at how fast twenty minutes passed. All too soon, Frances was announcing that the show would continue tomorrow. The red ON AIR light went off. They heard the familiar Earl's Auto Sales jingle playing through the speakers.

"I can't believe we just did a radio show!" Violet said as Gwen turned off the microphones. "I hope the listeners liked it."

As Violet spoke, the phones in the soundstage and Avery's control booth lit up.

Frances and Avery were busy answering one call after another.

Avery ran out of the control booth. "Kids love the program!"

"I wrote a hit show!" Frances crowed.

"Our actors deserve a lot of the credit," Avery said. "You were terrific!"

Frances took the next call. Jessie watched her happy smile turn into an expression of concern. Something was wrong.

When Frances hung up, she said, "Well, not *everyone* is thrilled with our show."

"Who was that?" Gwen asked.

"Earl Biggs," Frances said.

"The guy whose car commercials come on after the show?" Benny asked.

Frances nodded. "Exactly. He listened to the show from his office next door," she said. "He called to complain. He said he doesn't want to sponsor a kiddie show. Kids don't buy cars."

"He doesn't know the entire cast walked out yesterday," Avery said. "I'll tell him. And I'll tell him we're just doing a children's mystery program this week. And that the listeners loved it. Let's hope he isn't mad enough to pull his advertising."

"He seems to be looking for excuses to cancel his account," Frances said, leaving the room to answer another phone.

"Do you think it's possible that Earl could be the ghost?" Jessie asked Gwen.

Gwen looked sharply at her. "What makes you think that?"

"Everyone is a suspect in a case like this," Henry told her. "And Earl has a key, right? So he could sneak in and out without much trouble."

Gwen scowled. "I guess so." She turned abruptly from the Aldens and picked up the garbage can. "This place is a mess," she said. "I should clean."

"May we help?" asked Violet.

Gwen shrugged. "Sure. Gran can't afford a cleaning crew, so everyone who works here takes turns emptying the trash, mopping, and dusting."

"I'll sweep the floor," Jessie said.

"And I'll empty the trash cans," Benny offered.

"Thanks," said Gwen. "The Dumpster is out the side door."

Benny collected the trash in one wastebasket, then opened the door at the end of the hall. Benny didn't have a key, so he propped the door open with a second wastebasket.

A large Dumpster stood at the edge of the parking lot. On the other side was Earl's Auto Sales. The small cinder block building was surrounded by shiny cars.

As Benny watched, a man in a cowboy hat came out of the building. He walked over to one of the cars and slapped a SOLD sign under the windshield wiper.

When the man saw Benny, he crossed the parking lot.

"Don't believe I know you," he said in a gravelly voice. "I'm Earl Biggs."

"I'm Benny Alden," Benny replied.

The man's fluffy gray eyebrows shot upward in surprise. "You must be one of the kids in the radio show."

Benny nodded. "I was the ghost dog! My

brother and sisters are in the play, too. It's fun."

"Well, the fun's over," Earl said. "You won't be doing the show anymore. I need to talk to Avery." He walked into the station through the propped-open door.

Benny emptied the wastebasket, then hurried back inside the station. He heard a phone ringing. Both Avery and Frances were already tied up on other calls.

Benny spied an extension in the breakroom and picked up the receiver. Before he could say anything, he heard a man saying, "I *must* have an answer."

Benny's mouth dropped open in surprise. The gravelly voice sounded like Earl Biggs! Was he on another phone in the station?

Then another person spoke. "I need more time," she said.

Benny recognized the other voice, too. It was Jocelyn Hawley. She sounded upset.

What was Earl Biggs demanding from her?

CHAPTER 5

The Face in the Photograph

Before Benny could hear any more, Frances St. Clair swept into the breakroom.

"What are you doing?" she said sharply. "The station phones are not toys."

Benny quickly hung up the receiver. "It kept ringing, so I answered it."

"From now on," Frances said frostily, "let the grown-ups answer the phones."

She fetched a bottle of water from the refrigerator, then left without another word.

Why is she always so grouchy? Benny wondered.

Violet stuck her head in the door. "We're ready to go, Benny. How come you look so funny? Did something happen?"

Before Benny could reply, Frances came back in with Gwen. Gwen tidied the counter while they talked about the next day's show.

"Tell you later when we're alone," Benny whispered to Violet.

Gwen walked back to Jocelyn's house with them. She seemed distant. When they reached Jocelyn's, Gwen went straight to her bedroom and shut the door.

Grandfather and Jocelyn were in the office, studying a chart on the computer screen.

Henry, Jessie, Benny, and Violet settled on the couches in a small study upstairs. They were eager to discuss the mystery.

"Does anybody have anything to report?" Henry asked. "Suspicious behavior, clues . . ."

"Frances St. Clair might be a suspect," Violet said. "She doesn't like kids very much."

"A lot of people don't like children," Jessie pointed out. "That doesn't make them thieves."

"I think Frances is kind of strange, too," Henry said. "But why would she take the microphones and the records? What's her motive?"

"She doesn't seem to like writing the mystery show," Violet said. "Remember, she wanted to quit, too, when the cast left yesterday."

"I think Frances is just grumpy," Benny said. "My top suspect is Earl Biggs. And I have a clue!"

"Earl Biggs?" Jessie said. "We've never even seen him!"

"I have," Benny said. Benny told the others about meeting Earl by the Dumpster and the overheard phone call. "The woman was definitely Jocelyn. And I *think* the man was Earl Biggs!"

"Wow," said Henry. "This is major. What kind of answer do you think he needs from her?"

"Maybe Earl Biggs is trying to get Jocelyn to sell the station," Violet suggested.

Jessie nodded. "That would make Earl a strong suspect. And his auto shop is right next door to the station. He could easily sneak in and out during the day."

"He wasn't very nice, either," Benny said. "And he said we won't be doing the mystery show anymore! It sounded like a threat."

"We'll watch out for Earl Biggs," said Henry. "We could have this mystery wrapped up by tomorrow!"

After breakfast the next morning, Jessie, Violet, Henry, Benny, and Gwen left for the station.

"I have a feeling the 'ghost' will pay us a visit today," Gwen predicted as they walked down the street.

Henry patted his backpack. "I brought flashlights, just in case."

When they got to the station, Gwen and the Aldens waved hello to Avery, who was busy in the control booth, then went to the breakroom to wait for Frances to arrive with the script.

Gwen handed them each a paper cup filled with water. "Sipping water will help your voices," she advised.

Violet examined the framed photographs in the display case. "Do you know who these people are?" she asked Gwen.

"The cheerleader is Gran. That football player is my grandfather," said Gwen. "The other football player is Earl Biggs."

"Earl must be sad that Jocelyn married Luther instead of marrying him," Benny said.

Gwen shrugged. "That was a long time ago. I don't think he'd still be sad. Besides, Gran and Earl are good friends. And Earl was friends with my grandfather, too."

"Who's this girl?" Violet asked, pointing to a photograph of a girl with a ponytail, speaking into a microphone. "She's in all the radio station pictures."

"That," Gwen said, "is Daphne Owens."

"Really?" Violet looked at the pretty face more closely. "I wonder what happened to her . . ."

Just then, Frances walked briskly into the

breakroom. She nodded hello and handed each of them a script.

"You kids are good readers," she said. "I'll let you go over your lines by yourselves. Then we'll do the run-through."

Jessie, Henry, Benny, and Violet headed for the soundstage. As they passed the sound booth, Avery looked up and smiled. An opened box of chocolate doughnuts sat on the counter near his sports water bottle.

Jessie remembered Avery had a box of doughnuts on the console the day before, too. "Avery sure likes doughnuts," she said.

Benny tapped on the glass. He pointed to the doughnuts. That chocolate one sure looked good.

But Avery, who was talking into the mike, shook his head.

"He doesn't want to share," Benny said, disappointed.

"Maybe he didn't know what you wanted," said Jessie. "Anyway, you just had breakfast."

"I think it's a little strange," Violet remarked. "Usually Avery is so nice. He can't eat all those doughnuts himself."

"He ate all the doughnuts yesterday," Jessie said, opening the door to the soundstage. "Maybe those doughnuts are Avery's breakfast and lunch."

Henry pulled up four folding chairs. "I wish we had time to memorize our lines," he said, "in case the lights go out."

"I could! I only have to remember 'woof' and 'arf,'" Benny said, making them all laugh.

Then Gwen came in. "How's the script?"

"Today's episode is really good," Jessie said. "Our characters get caught outside in a storm. They see the ghost dog in a graveyard on a hill, and he leads them to shelter and then disappears."

"When they go into the graveyard again, they find a tombstone with the dog's picture on it," Violet added.

Gwen looked over her own copy of the script. "Hmmm. I'll need my thunderstorm tape. I can make the wind sound effects with a fan."

After Gwen had assembled her props,

the cast did a run-through with Frances.

"Fine," she said crisply. "You're ready to go on the air."

The kids began the live show at ten o'clock. Everything was going well until the windstorm scene. Right after Gwen turned on her fan, the lights flickered, then died. Only the red ON AIR light remained on.

"Don't stop!" Henry whispered to the others, clicking on his flashlight.

Violet and Jessie turned on their flashlights, too. Without a pause, they read their parts as if nothing was wrong.

At least this time there isn't any horrible screaming, Jessie thought. She aimed her flashlight around the soundstage. She saw the fan on Gwen's stool, still blowing mightily. But Gwen wasn't at her station. Before she could beam her flashlight into the shadow-draped corners, the lights came back on.

Avery, who was just entering his booth, gave them a thumbs-up signal through the soundproof glass. Frances paced in the hallway.

Then Jessie noticed that Gwen was at her station, changing tapes in front of her microphone. Had she been in the room all along, hidden in the shadows?

Henry, Jessie, Violet, and Benny exchanged eyebrow-raised glances, but they kept going through the last scene in the play. At last the show ended. Avery cued up the Earl's Auto Sales commercial and came into the soundstage.

"You kids were terrific," he praised. "You too, Gwen. It was great how you kept the play going even when the lights went out. You're just like professionals!"

"What happened?" Gwen asked breathlessly.

Jessie stared at her. Why was Gwen short of breath? Had she left the room, then hurried back under cover of darkness? Or had the incident genuinely frightened her?

"Some of the fuses were pulled," Avery said. "Whoever is doing this knows our fuse box is by the side door. And he knows exactly which fuses to loosen to make the lights go out."

"What do you mean?" Benny asked, confused.

"The fuse box in the hall controls the electricity in the station," Avery explained. "One fuse is for the electricity to my equipment. Another fuse controls the lights. Still another controls the microwave and refrigerator in the breakroom. So to make the lights go out, the ghost has to pull the right fuse."

"The fan stayed on," Jessie pointed out, "and so did the red ON AIR light. Those fuses weren't touched."

Avery nodded. "The equipment stayed on, too. The commercial is about over. I'd better start some music."

Avery dashed back to the sound booth. Suddenly he cried out. The Aldens, Frances, and Gwen ran into the control booth.

Avery stood before the counter, holding up several frayed cables.

"The turntable!" he exclaimed. "It's gone!"

"You didn't see this before?" Henry asked.

"No!" Avery said. "I punched a button on this side to play the commercial. I didn't even look over here where the turntable is plugged in."

Frances put her hand to her mouth. "Someone stole it! We were both in the back working on the fuse box, but surely we would have heard something."

"Not necessarily," said Violet. "That fan made a lot of noise. And we were still broadcasting."

"I didn't hear anything," Gwen said — a little too quickly, Jessie thought. "I'm going to pack up my sound effects stuff," she added, and left.

Avery sighed. "I can use the CD changer for now, but a lot of our best music is on records. Jocelyn will have to buy a new turntable. That won't make her happy."

A gravelly voice spoke from the hall. "What won't make Jocelyn happy?"

Henry turned to see a tall man in a black cowboy hat standing in the doorway. He held a key ring loosely in his fingers.

"Hello, Earl," said Frances.

So that's Earl Biggs, Henry thought.

"Nobody answered my question," Earl said.

"We had another robbery," Avery told him. "The turntable was stolen this time."

Earl shook his head. "Tough luck. I know that equipment is expensive."

Avery seemed annoyed. "Did you come over for a reason, Earl?"

"Yes," said the older man. "Is Jocelyn here?"

"No," Avery said, sighing.

"Oh," said Earl. "Well, I . . . I, uh, I thought I told you to stop running that kid-die show."

"But it's popular," Frances said. "Watch, the calls from kids will be coming in any second."

"I don't care," Earl said. "Kids don't buy cars. Put on the regular program!"

"We can't," Avery said. "You know the cast from the diner quit. We're lucky to have the Aldens fill in for them."

Benny stared at the key ring in Earl Biggs's hand. "Is that a key to the side door?"

"Yup," Earl replied. "Jocelyn gave me a key. My office is right next door." Earl attached the key ring to his belt. "I'm a . . . a family friend."

"You're only supposed to use that key in emergencies," Avery said tightly.

Earl shrugged. "It hardly seems to matter. Somebody — or *something* — is coming into this station anytime he or she wants."

While Avery, Frances, and Earl argued, the Aldens slipped out the side door Earl had used. Again, Benny propped it open with a wastebasket.

"Let's split up and look for clues," Jessie told the others. "If Earl stole the turntable, he didn't have much time to stash it."

Violet and Benny went around the side of the building. Jessie started peeking under the cars in the parking lot. Henry stood still and looked around him.

"The Dumpster!" Henry said to himself. "It's a perfect hiding place!"

Before he could cross the parking lot, Henry saw a figure dart around the corner of the building. He caught a glimpse of long red hair. "Gwen?" Henry called. The only answer came from a mockingbird perched on the roof.

Henry ran around the back of the radio station but saw no one. Entering by the front door, he saw Gwen in the hall between the soundstage and the control booth.

"Were you outside just now?" Henry asked.

"I've been in here, emptying the trash," she replied, tying the ends of a plastic garbage sack. Her long hair fell over her face like a curtain. Henry couldn't tell if she was telling the truth.

Jessie, Violet, and Benny came back inside just as Gwen disappeared into the breakroom.

"What's up?" Benny asked Henry.

"We have another suspect," Henry declared. "Jocelyn's own granddaughter!"

CHAPTER 6

The Ghost Prowls at Night

"The show sounded great today," Jocelyn praised. She and Grandfather had dropped by the station and found Henry, Jessie, Violet, and Benny in the breakroom.

Avery came in, joined by Gwen and Frances. "Well, these kids kept it going but it wasn't easy," he said. "The 'ghost' visited again."

"Is something missing?" Grandfather asked.

"The turntable," Gwen replied.

Jocelyn sighed. "That turntable was expensive. Our thief knows exactly what to take."

"Don't you think you should report these robberies to the police?" Grandfather asked.

Jocelyn sighed. "I guess I'd better — "

"No!" Gwen cried. "I mean, the police might scare the ghost away."

"Wouldn't that be good?" Violet asked.

"Yeah, but we might not get the equipment back," Gwen said.

Henry's right, Violet thought. *Sometimes Gwen acts like she* doesn't *want this case solved*.

"I'll have to buy a replacement turntable in Port City," Jocelyn said. "That's the nearest town that carries them."

"We could drive there right now," Grandfather suggested. He turned to Gwen. "Why don't you kids relax, then eat at the diner this evening? You've all been working hard on the radio program."

The Aldens spent the rest of the afternoon strolling around Deer Crossing. Gwen didn't want to go. She said she wanted to stay home to read.

After playing in the park, the Aldens went back to Jocelyn's house. Gwen was waiting impatiently. "It's time to go eat," she said.

"Was your book good?" Benny asked.

"What book? Oh," Gwen corrected herself. "Yes, I finished it."

Jessie wondered what Gwen had *really* been doing.

The children walked to the Route 11 Diner and settled into a booth near a window. The only other customer was a man in a dark suit sitting at a table in the back.

DeeDee was their waitress again. She wore a blue ribbon on her collar.

"Seen that ghost anymore?" she asked, pulling her pencil from her apron pocket.

"The lights went out while we were broadcasting today's show," Jessie said. "And the turntable was missing."

"Daphne Owens strikes again!" DeeDee seemed almost pleased.

"It can't be a ghost," said Violet. "Ghosts can't lift heavy objects."

"Ghosts can do anything," DeeDee stated. "You know what you want yet?"

Everyone ordered burgers with fries and vanilla shakes. DeeDee brought their food promptly.

"You kids are awful brave to stay at that station," she said, plunking down the ketchup bottle. "Who knows what that ghost will do next!" She bustled off to wait on customers at the counter.

"How can DeeDee actually believe in that ghost story?" Henry said.

Jessie dragged a french fry through a pool of ketchup. "It's weird. Grown-ups should know better." Then she had a thought. "Unless DeeDee is just fooling with us."

"DeeDee is new to Deer Crossing, right?" Henry said.

"She just moved here," said Gwen, nodding. "Nobody knows much about her."

"How long has she worked at the station?" Violet wanted to know.

"About two months," Gwen replied.

"When did the ghost first show up?" Benny asked.

"A little over a month ago," said Gwen. "What are you getting at?"

Henry looked thoughtful. "Did the ghost ever appear *before* DeeDee came to the station?"

"Funny little things would happen," Gwen said. "Like, the mike cords would get tangled. We'd joke that it was Daphne's ghost." She stopped. "Do you think Dee-Dee is the ghost?"

"She knows her way around the station," Henry said. "And she seems pretty intent on spreading the ghost story."

"Yes, but it would be harder for her to pull these pranks now that she doesn't work at the show," Violet pointed out.

"Still," said Jessie. "She does seem awfully interested in this mystery."

"We can't rule out anyone as a suspect," Benny said. *Not even Gwen*, he thought.

While the children were eating, Avery walked into the diner. He was dressed in running clothes. Without looking around, he headed straight to the back and sat down across from the man in the dark suit. The two men began talking.

"He didn't even see us," Benny commented.

"Do you know that man Avery's with?" Jessie asked Gwen.

Gwen shook her head. "I've never seen him before."

DeeDee, who was refilling the salt shaker at the next booth, said, "That man has been coming in here a lot this month."

"Who is he?" asked Violet.

"He told me he's a businessman," DeeDee replied. "He doesn't live in Deer Crossing. Sometimes he and Avery eat dinner together."

But that night, the men were not eating. The waitress named Gayle brought them a pot of coffee and poured two cups. When she left, Avery and the dark-suited stranger returned to their quiet discussion.

"I wonder what they're talking about," Violet said. "They look awfully serious."

DeeDee put one hand on her hip. "Once when I waited on them, I overheard the man telling Avery, 'I could make you a star.' "

"How could he make Avery a star?" asked Violet.

"I don't know," DeeDee replied. "They quit talking when I served their food. My theory is, the man is really a talent scout, like the one that visited the radio station years ago."

"Avery is just a DJ," said Jessie. "How could a talent scout make him famous?"

"There are famous DJs," Gwen said. "But they usually work at radio stations in big cities."

"Maybe the man is just an old friend," Henry said.

"Maybe," said DeeDee. "But he and Avery don't ever laugh or anything. They just talk very seriously." She glanced at the two men, who still hadn't looked over at the Aldens' table. "Well, I'd better get back to work."

Gwen finished her burger in silence. Then she stood up. "I left my backpack at the station. I'll see you guys back at the house."

Through the side window, Violet watched Gwen cross the parking lot. "That's funny," she said. "I don't remember Gwen taking a bag this morning."

"Maybe she wanted to go back to the station to catch the ghost all by herself," Benny suggested.

"Maybe," said Henry. "Or maybe Gwen *is* the ghost."

"If that's true," said Violet, "Gwen could be going back for the turntable."

"But why would she do this to her own grandmother?" Jessie asked.

The door opened, jingling the cowbells tied to the handle. Frances St. Clair walked in and claimed a stool at the counter.

Shielded by the high leather sides of their booth, the Aldens were hidden from Frances's view. But they could hear her clearly.

"Coffee, please," Frances told DeeDee. "Make it strong. I've still got to finish tomorrow's script."

"I thought you wrote the radio script during the day," DeeDee said.

Frances lowered her voice, but the Aldens could still hear her. "Don't tell anyone, but I worked on my movie script today. Usually I write that at home, but I had this really great idea for a new script and couldn't wait to start working on it."

"What's it about?" DeeDee asked.

Frances sounded excited. "It's a mystery. I got the idea from the children's show we're doing this week, which is about a ghost dog. And of course we have that old ghost story at the station — "

"Are you sure it's just a story?" DeeDee said mysteriously. The Alden children looked at each other.

Frances paused, then went on. "Anyway, my movie will be about a long-dead radio actor who comes back to haunt the station. I'm sure Hollywood will snap up my script! I'll be rich!"

DeeDee gave a short laugh. "Yeah, right!"

"You laugh now," Frances said haughtily. "But one day I'll be famous! People won't laugh then. And I'll be through writing silly radio jingles."

"I wouldn't mind writing for the radio," DeeDee said wistfully. "It would be better than waitressing."

"When I quit, you can have my job,"

Frances said. "But until I have enough money to go to California, I'll have to stay here."

The children waited until Frances left the diner, then paid their bill. They walked slowly toward the Hawley house.

"Frances really wants to be rich and famous," said Jessie.

"Who doesn't?" Benny asked.

"I'd rather be happy," Henry said. "Money doesn't always make a person happy. But Frances needs enough money to move to Hollywood. She could be stealing the equipment and selling it."

Jessie nodded. "That makes sense. It could easily be Frances. The thief obviously knows his — or her — way around the station."

"The ghost either works at the station," Henry added, "or used to."

"Daphne Owens wanted to be rich and famous," Violet said. "She was going to be a star."

Jessie stopped. "Do you think there's a connection between Daphne and Frances?"

"How could there be?" Henry asked. "Daphne worked at WCXZ a long time ago and then she disappeared. Frances probably wasn't even born then."

"Do you suppose Frances is haunting the station to get a good story for her movie?" Jessie suggested.

"Maybe," said Violet. "We'll have to keep an eye on her."

Benny was staring at something. "There's Frances," he said, pointing to someone sitting on a bench in the park they were passing. "And isn't that Gwen hiding behind a bush?"

"It *is* Gwen," Henry confirmed.

"What is she doing?" Jessie wondered. "She said she was going back to the station for her backpack."

"She looks like she's spying on Frances," said Violet.

Benny cupped his hands around his mouth. "Gwen!"

Gwen stood up, looking around nervously. Frances hadn't noticed her. Gwen crossed the street and walked toward the

Aldens. "I thought you guys would be home already," she said, scowling.

"We thought you went back to the station," said Jessie. "Why were you in the park?"

"I was taking a shortcut home," Gwen answered huffily. "Look, there's my grandmother's car. They must be back." Without waiting for the Aldens, she ran toward the house.

"That's weird," said Henry. "She's not carrying a backpack."

"Gwen is *definitely* up to something," Benny said. He opened the front door of Jocelyn's house and they went inside.

"Did you get the new turntable?" Gwen asked her grandmother.

"Yes, and it cost even more than I thought it would," said Jocelyn. "I'm going to make some hot tea. Are there any of those oatmeal cookies left?"

"I'll make the tea," Gwen offered. "You go relax in the living room."

"May we take a walk?" Henry asked Grandfather. "It's such a nice evening."

Grandfather checked the mantel clock. "It's pretty late. Don't be gone long."

The Alden children strolled down Main Street. Only the diner was still open. The town was quiet, except for an occasional car passing through.

"We've walked all the way to the radio station," Benny said.

"Look!" Jessie said in a hushed voice. "Aren't those lights in the back window?"

"It's after eight o'clock," Violet said. "The station is closed for the night. Who could be in there?"

"Let's check it out," Henry said. "I have the key." He unlocked the front door and flipped on the lights. The kids looked in every room, but found no one.

"We must have seen the reflection of a car's headlights," Jessie concluded.

Or the ghost of Daphne Owens, Benny thought. He knew ghosts didn't really exist, but the thought made him shiver.

CHAPTER 7

The Missing Script

Back at the Hawley house, the Alden kids met Gwen on the porch. She was out of breath.

"Hi, Gwen," Benny said. "What are you doing?"

Gwen looked startled to see them. A guilty look passed over her face. "I, uh, I was just looking for you guys," Gwen said unconvincingly. "Let's go inside."

As they followed Gwen inside the house, the Aldens exchanged glances. Had Gwen really been looking for them, or was she out of breath because she had just run home from the station? If so, what had she been doing there?

They said good night to Grandfather and Jocelyn, then headed upstairs to bed.

"Sleep well," Henry told the others. "Tomorrow's another big day."

Jessie nodded. "I'll say. If that *was* the 'ghost' at the station, I bet tomorrow there will be another haunting."

"Either way," Benny concluded, "it looks like Gwen Hawley is our number one suspect."

"I've outdone myself," Frances St. Clair bragged as she passed out the new script. "Today's episode is even better than yesterday's." She helped herself to some coffee, then left the room.

Henry, Jessie, and Violet sat down and read the script. Benny watched the rain streaming down the breakroom window.

"Wow," Henry said. "This is exciting stuff. The kids get a dog that runs away, so they go hunting for him — "

"And the ghost dog leads them into an old house in the woods," Jessie added. "Today we end with another storm and our characters are trapped in an old mine. I wonder what will happen tomorrow?"

At that moment, Gwen came in with a box of cassette tapes. She had overheard Jessie's last remark.

"Nobody knows, not even Frances," she said. "That's the way she works. She doesn't even know the ending until it's time for her to write it."

"I get to do a lot of barking today," Benny told Gwen. "I play the real dog *and* the ghost dog."

"You'd better practice two different kinds of barks," Gwen said. "Let's go to the soundstage. It's almost time for the run-through."

The run-through went smoothly. Gwen made note of the sound effects she'd have to do, like strong winds blowing and creaking floorboards in the old house. "I'll need a lot of tapes today," she said, going through her box.

Avery waved, inviting them into the control booth. "Hi," he said. "Are you ready for today? I think every kid in Deer Crossing is tuning in to your show now."

"We're having a lot of fun," Jessie told him.

Henry pointed. "Is that the new turntable?" he asked.

"Yup," Avery said. "It's a nice one. Jocelyn brought it by early this morning."

Jessie nodded. "She said it cost even more than she'd expected."

"Really?" said Avery. "That's too bad. I know Jocelyn has been worried about money. Do you think she might sell the station?"

"She seems determined not to," Henry said.

"She won't have to," Benny said, "because we're going to catch the ghost."

Jessie noticed Avery's duffel bag in the corner. "Are you still going to run today, even though it's raining?"

"Yes," Avery said. "I run in all types of weather. This job involves a lot of sitting. I need the exercise."

Earl Biggs came down the hall, jingling his keys.

"You're not doing that kiddie show again, are you?" Earl asked Avery. "I'd rather you played tapes of the old shows."

"You don't run this station," Avery told him. "Jocelyn does."

"Hmph," said Earl. "We'll see."

It was almost time to broadcast the show. The Aldens went into the breakroom to fill four cups with water. Gwen was there buying a juice from the vending machine. They walked to the soundstage together.

Frances had placed the Aldens' microphones in a row. Gwen's microphone stood farther back, next to the stool holding her prop box, cassette player, and the tapes she had taken out for the show.

Frances checked to make sure everyone was ready, then counted them down. They were on the air.

"Ow-oooooo," Benny howled into Violet's microphone, playing the ghost dog.

Frances gave Gwen the cue for the first sound effect, a door creaking open. Gwen punched the button on her cassette player.

"Meow! Meow! Me —"

Gwen quickly hit the STOP button. Frances frowned, but cued Henry, who had the first line.

"What was that?" Henry said. "It sounded like a wolf."

Jessie lowered her voice dramatically. "Do you think it was that strange white dog we keep seeing?"

It was time for the sound of someone walking up squeaky stairs. Gwen put the next tape into the cassette player and punched the ON button.

Rrrrrrr. This time a lawn mower noise blasted from the machine.

Rattled, Gwen hit STOP. She scrabbled through her tapes.

Through the window, Jessie saw Earl Biggs pacing impatiently.

Frances waved her hands as if to say, "Forget it." They would have to do the show without any taped sound effects. Gwen got out the men's shoes to make footsteps.

The Aldens performed their parts well until Jessie's microphone quit.

She tapped it lightly, but it was dead. She moved over by Violet to share hers.

Then Henry's mike went dead! He stood by Violet and Jessie. Now all three shared the same mike. It remained working for the rest of the program.

At last the show was over.

"What a disaster!" Frances exclaimed. "What else could have gone wrong? Gwen, what happened with your tapes?"

Gwen was nearly in tears. "I don't know! I put them in order right after the run-through."

"Somebody obviously went through your box and switched the tape labels," said Violet. "When could they have done it?"

"I left the soundstage after arranging my tapes," Gwen said, "to go to the breakroom for some juice. But I was only gone a minute."

"It takes longer than a minute to switch labels," Violet said.

"Frances, did you see anyone?" Jessie asked.

Frances shook her head. "No, but I wasn't in the room the whole time."

Gwen still looked shaken. "If I didn't know better, I might start to believe in this ghost."

Henry was following the trail of microphone cords to the wall sockets. "Violet's and Jessie's mikes were only plugged in partway," he announced. "That was dangerous — they could have shorted."

"This ghost," Gwen said, "means business."

They walked out of the soundstage and into the hall.

"Sorry about today's show," Avery apologized to Earl. "We had technical difficulties. But the Aldens still did a great job."

Earl looked around. "Is Jocelyn coming today?"

"Probably," said Avery.

Benny noticed a small flashlight hanging from the key chain on Earl's belt. Was Earl the visitor last night? Did he sneak into the station and loosen the plugs on the microphones? Did he mess up Gwen's tapes?

Grandfather and Jocelyn pushed open the lobby door.

When Earl saw Jocelyn, he asked her, "Are you free now?" Benny watched Earl. He had a funny expression on his face.

"Sorry," Jocelyn said to Earl. "Not now. James and I are taking the children out to lunch."

Earl left, looking disappointed.

On the way to the diner, Violet thought about the old photo in the breakroom. "Was that really Earl Biggs in the picture of the football game? It doesn't look like him."

"Yes, that's Earl," Jocelyn replied with a laugh. "He had more hair back then."

"Earl sure hangs around the station a lot," Benny said.

Jocelyn smiled. "He's an important advertiser — and an important friend."

"I think Earl still has a crush on you, Jocelyn," Violet said cautiously.

Jocelyn looked surprised. Then she blushed. "You might be right, Violet. Earl has been pressuring me to date him again.

I told him I need some time to think about it — I'm not sure I'm ready for that."

So that explained the mushy look on Earl's face, Benny thought. *Earl was in love with Jocelyn.*

Benny exchanged glances with his brother and sisters. So that's what Earl had been asking Jocelyn on the phone!

After they were seated, Frances came into the diner. "I'm getting my lunch to go," she told Jocelyn, stopping by their table. "I'm going back to the station to work on the last installment of the show. What better place to write a ghost story than in a haunted station?" She laughed.

Jessie nudged Henry. "Let's go back, too," she whispered, "to look for more clues."

Henry nodded. "We're running out of time. Tomorrow's our last day on the show."

Raindrops dripped off the trees. It had stopped raining, but jagged clouds sailed across the sky.

The Aldens didn't tell Gwen they were going back to the station. Jocelyn's granddaughter went up to her room right after they returned to the house, claiming she had a headache.

The Aldens walked into the station just as Avery turned off the long record he'd been playing and sat down to announce the day's news.

"Let's check out the soundstage," Henry suggested. "Maybe we'll find clues we've overlooked."

As the Aldens walked into the hallway, Benny grabbed Violet's sleeve.

"What is it?" she said.

Benny pointed at the side door. "I hear noises," he whispered. "Somebody's out there!"

Before the Aldens could investigate, Frances St. Clair ran out of the breakroom.

"My script!" she cried. "It's been stolen!"

CHAPTER 8

Violet's Big Clue

"Tell us exactly what happened," Henry said to Frances.

"I had just finished writing the script," Frances said. "I went into the rest room to wash the ink off my fingers. When I came back, the script was gone! I don't know how this could have happened — Avery and I are the only ones here."

"This just happened," Jessie said. "The thief can't be far."

"The side door!" Benny said. "Remember? I just heard someone out there!"

"That has to be the thief's escape route," Jessie said. "Hurry before he gets away!"

The Aldens dashed forward. Frances stood where she was, wringing her hands. She seemed too distraught to move.

Jessie reached the end of the hall first. She unbolted the inside lock and flung open the door.

Just beyond the doorway, a figure was crouched in the shadows. The person sprang up to run away.

"Stop!" Henry commanded.

The figure stepped into the light. It was Gwen Hawley.

"Gwen!" exclaimed Violet. "What are you doing here?"

Gwen looked embarrassed. "I came back here to look for clues," she said.

"Clues?" asked Jessie.

Gwen nodded sheepishly. "I want to help Gran by finding the ghost. I thought I could be a detective, too. I even followed you guys to the station last night. That time you saw me in the park, I was following Frances. I thought she might be the thief.

She's trying to earn enough money to go to California."

The Aldens looked at one another. "Does this mean you didn't steal tomorrow's script?" Benny said.

Gwen looked shocked. "Steal the script? No! I was looking for clues out back."

Henry believed her. "Well, did you see anyone out here who might have? Frances says somebody took it just a few minutes ago."

"Oh, no!" said Gwen. "No, I didn't see anyone."

"The thief must have used this door," Henry said, "because we came through the front door. But the door was locked — whoever used it had to have a key."

"Earl has a key," said Gwen. "So does Frances. And Avery."

"If Earl Biggs took it, he's already gotten away," said Violet. "If it was Frances or Avery, they're both still here — the script could be hidden in the station, or dropped somewhere out here."

Jessie spoke in a near whisper. "If Frances

is the thief, she could be hiding the script right now. Maybe that's why she didn't follow us outside."

Just then, Frances stepped out of the station. "I didn't see anyone in there," she said.

"Let's look around out here," Benny said.

The Aldens, Gwen, and Frances fanned out to search.

Jessie glanced at the office of the Auto Sales lot. She wondered if Earl Biggs was the 'ghost' — he could be making trouble at the station to get Jocelyn's attention. Maybe he had sneaked in the side door with his key, hidden in the shadows until Frances left the breakroom, then grabbed the script and gone out the side door. Gwen had been outside behind the station, so she wouldn't have seen him.

"I don't think we're going to find it," Frances said after they had searched a while. "I'll just have to write the whole script over." She sighed. "It'll take me hours."

"We'll help," Henry offered. "With all of us working, it won't take so long."

"I can't write very well," Benny said. "But I can staple the pages together."

Frances smiled gratefully. "Thanks, Benny. You five are lifesavers."

They sat down at the table in the breakroom and got to work. Because Frances had just written the script, she remembered most of it. She told the story while Jessie, Violet, and Henry copied it down. Gwen wrote the sound effects directions.

It was almost dinnertime before they finished. Avery put on a prerecorded program, changed into his running clothes, and put his work clothes in the closet. "Is everything ready for tomorrow?" he asked as the Aldens walked by the sound booth.

"Yup," Henry said. "The final script is great."

"Good," said Avery. He picked up his duffel bag and headed for the door.

Frances came in with her raincoat over one arm. "I just spoke with Jocelyn. She and Mr. Alden and Earl Biggs are all coming to tomorrow's broadcast."

Avery paused. "If nothing goes wrong

with the show, maybe Earl won't cancel his advertising."

"Tomorrow's show *must* go right," Violet said.

Frances opened the lobby door. "Avery, do you need a ride?"

"No, thanks," he said. "I'm going running as always."

Frances turned to the Aldens and Gwen. "Jocelyn asked me to tell you you'll be eating dinner late tonight. She suggested that you stop by the diner for a snack."

"Sounds good to me," Benny said. "I ate ages ago."

Henry grinned. "It wasn't *that* long ago. But I could go for some ice cream."

They followed Frances outside and said good-bye as she climbed into her rusty old car. "When I'm rich and famous in Hollywood," she declared, "I'll buy a brand-new car." She waved and smiled. "See you tomorrow!"

The diner was nearly empty when the children walked in.

DeeDee motioned them over to a large booth and signaled that she would be with them in a minute.

"Time is running out. We only have *one day* to solve this mystery," Henry reminded the others.

"None of our suspects has a strong motive," Violet said. "We've ruled out Gwen. Yes, you were a suspect until tonight."

"That leaves Frances, Avery, and Earl," said Jessie. "I think Frances is the most suspicious. She wants to write a movie script, and she could be playing the ghost to help her with her story."

"But she seems to like the kids' show she's writing," Henry pointed out. "Why would she sabotage it?"

"Frances and Avery are both key suspects," Violet said. "They both have keys to the station and they're around every day. Either one of them could be stealing stuff to sell for the money."

"But then they'd be out of a job," Henry pointed out. "That doesn't make sense."

"That leaves Earl," said Gwen. "He keeps

telling Gran he's going to cancel his account."

Jessie had been thinking. "I don't believe he will," she said, "or he would have done it by now. I think Earl says that to get your grandmother's attention. Remember, he really likes her."

"Jessie's right," Violet put in. "Earl keeps coming into the station to try to talk to her. I think he just uses his advertisements as an excuse to be there."

"Boy," said Gwen admiringly. "You guys are good."

An idea slowly formed in Violet's mind. "You know," she said, "maybe we should think more about the old mystery."

Benny frowned. "What old mystery?"

"The one about Daphne Owens," Jessie said. "She's supposed to be the ghost. What *really* happened to her? She didn't vanish into thin air."

"If she moved to another town, maybe we can find her — you know, by looking in phone books or something," Gwen said, pulling napkins from the dispenser.

"She'd be hard to find," Henry put in. "She might have gotten married and changed her last name."

"She could be anywhere," Benny said glumly.

DeeDee came over with her order pad. She wore pink and yellow ribbons in a bow at her neck. "What would you like tonight?"

"Your ribbons are pretty," Gwen complimented.

DeeDee touched the bow. "Thank you. I've been wearing ribbons every day since I was your age. My hair was long then, like yours. I always wore it in a ponytail tied with a ribbon. After I left my hometown and got married, I cut my hair. But I still wear ribbons."

As Violet listened to DeeDee, she thought about the other person in Deer Crossing who always wore a ribbon in her ponytail — the girl in the photographs at the station: Daphne Owens. She remembered the talent scout remark DeeDee had made. Who else was so interested in talent scouts? *It can't be*, Violet thought. But somehow it made sense.

"DeeDee!" she exclaimed. "You're Daphne Owens!"

The others looked at Violet in surprise.

DeeDee nearly dropped her pad and pencil. "What did you say?"

"I said, you're Daphne Owens," said Violet. "You've changed your name. But it's you."

"Well, I'll be — " DeeDee gave her bark of a laugh. "I never thought anybody would figure it out. Too bad. It was such fun, working in the radio station again with everyone thinking I was a ghost. My little joke."

"So is Rhoads your married name?" Gwen asked.

"Yes," DeeDee said. "And DeeDee is a nickname. After my husband died, I moved back to Deer Crossing. But since nobody remembered me, I didn't tell them who I really was. I like having secrets."

"Why did you leave Deer Crossing in the

first place?" Henry wanted to know. "Was it really because of the talent scout?"

"Yes. I was so embarrassed," said Dee-Dee. "I had bragged to everyone about how I was going to be a star. And then the show was a disaster! I had made a fool of myself. How could I face my friends?"

"So you left town that day," Jessie said.

DeeDee nodded. "I only meant to go away for a little while — I thought I would come back to Deer Crossing once my embarrassment died down. But then I met Harold Rhoads. We fell in love and were married." DeeDee smiled. "He called me DeeDee. I kept the name, even after I moved back here."

Benny had the most important question. He looked at the waitress and asked boldly, "Are you haunting the radio station?"

CHAPTER 9

A Simple Solution

"Do you believe I'm the ghost of WCXZ?" DeeDee asked him.

Benny frowned. "Ghosts aren't real. But *somebody* is stealing stuff from the radio station."

Henry spoke up. "DeeDee, I think you like having people believe the ghost of Daphne Owens is haunting the station. In a way, it's like you're the star you always wanted to be."

"You're very smart," DeeDee said. "And you're right, Henry. I *do* like the attention.

I guess that's why I kept saying Daphne's ghost was back. I like it that people here remember me."

"But you're not the one causing the trouble at the station," Jessie stated.

DeeDee shook her head. "I've never stolen anything in my life. And I never dreamed I would cause the whole cast to quit. I guess I just got carried away. I really like doing the radio show. I hope I can go back."

"Then why don't you tell my grandmother?" Gwen said. "And talk to the others here at the diner so they'll come back, too. If the show goes off the air, my grandmother will be crushed."

"The station may not be haunted, but spooky things *are* happening," said DeeDee. "Until the real 'ghost' is caught, the cast won't come back, no matter what I tell them."

"We'll find the ghost," Violet said.

As they gathered their things, Jessie mused, "It seems like everyone wants to be a star. Frances wants to be a famous movie writer. DeeDee — Daphne — wanted to be a famous radio actress."

Gwen smiled sheepishly. "And I wanted to be a famous detective — or, at least, to figure out this mystery."

"Let's go over the facts again," said Henry. "We know that the ghost must be someone who knows the station well. He knows where to find the light switches and fuse box and exactly what to take."

"Right," said Jessie. "And it's probably someone who is around the station a lot anyway — if it were an outsider, like DeeDee, how would she get in and out without anyone seeing her?"

"But if it's an insider, like Avery or Frances, how is the 'ghost' getting the stolen stuff out?" said Violet.

Gwen was looking out the window. "There goes Avery on his evening run," she said. "I wonder why he's carrying that duffel bag."

"Gwen!" Jessie exclaimed. "That's it!"

"What's it?" said Benny.

"The solution to the mystery," Jessie said.

"We keep thinking the thief leaves the station, like when we were looking for Frances's script. What if he comes and goes, carrying something we see every day?"

"Of course!" said Gwen, smiling. "The duffel bag! That must be it."

Henry was smiling, too. "It's just like your best sound effects, Gwen — very simple."

As they walked home from the diner, the Aldens and Gwen figured out a plan to catch the ghost.

The next day, Grandfather and Jocelyn drove the kids to the station. On the way, they stopped at the diner to pick up a dozen doughnuts. "To celebrate the final episode," Jocelyn said.

When they reached the station, Earl Biggs was already inside, pacing back and forth in the lobby.

"I'm glad you made it," Jocelyn said to him.

Earl held open the door for them. "I was glad to come."

The Aldens and Gwen went into the breakroom.

"I am so nervous," Frances said, handing out the scripts. "I never thought I'd be so nervous about a kiddie show. But this has turned out to be one of the best stories I've ever written. The final episode has to go perfectly today!"

"It will," Jessie reassured her.

Avery walked into the breakroom. "You guys brought doughnuts, too."

"You can have one if you want." Benny selected one with chocolate icing.

"No, thanks. I brought my own, as usual." Avery rinsed his coffee mug.

Because the kids had helped rewrite the final script, they already knew the story. It didn't take them long to go over their parts. Benny helped Gwen sort through her sound tapes. After they had set aside all the tapes they would need during the broadcast, Gwen took out a blank tape. Then she and Benny recorded one more sound effect they would need for the show.

"Perfect," Benny said to Gwen. "Now

we have everything we need to catch the ghost."

Gwen placed the tape to one side of the cassette player. She looked up at Henry, Jessie, and Violet and nodded. Everything for their plan was set.

At last it was show time.

"Ready, everyone?" Frances called. The kids nodded. "Places, everyone! One, two, three! You're on the air!"

The red ON AIR light blinked on.

Frances read the introduction. "In part three," she said into Jessie's mike, "our characters were trapped in the old mine. Will the mysterious dog help them again? We'll find out today in the final episode of 'The Ghost Dog.'"

Violet had the first line. "Don't move, anyone, or the rocks will come down!"

"My leg is stuck," said Henry with a groan. "I can't get it free."

"Oh, no!" cried Jessie. "Watch out — !"

Gwen shook a metal box with a few pebbles inside. It sounded just like rocks falling down the mine shaft.

Moments into the broadcast, the lights went out. The soundstage was completely dark. This time the kids didn't click on their flashlights. They had memorized their parts so they wouldn't need them.

Screeeeeeeeeeeeee! A horrible, loud screeching filled the radio station.

The Aldens continued to recite their lines, pretending the screaming was part of the show.

In the darkness, Gwen picked up the cassette she and Benny had made earlier and slid it into the cassette player.

"Is that the ghost dog?" Violet said loud enough to be heard over the screeching.

Gwen pushed the PLAY button on the cassette player. The howls of a dog — Benny's character of the ghost dog — competed with the screaming.

"Go, Benny!" Gwen whispered to him.

"Wish me luck!" he whispered back, then crept around the back of the soundstage.

The plan relied on him. He couldn't fail.

The ON AIR light cast an eerie glow as Benny edged out the door of the sound-

stage. He waited a few seconds for his eyes
to adjust to the dim red light.

Holding on to the wall, Benny shuffled
down the hall that connected the soundstage to the rest of the studio. He could
hear Grandfather and Jocelyn coming out
of the breakroom.

"What's going on?" Jocelyn yelled. "Somebody stop that noise!"

"We have to get the lights back on!"
Grandfather told her.

The fuse box was near the side door,
Benny knew. They would head in that direction.

Then Benny saw a dark shape ahead of
him.

Taking the flashlight out of his pocket,
Benny clicked the button to the ON position
and aimed the beam straight at the "ghost."

"Stop right there," Benny said.

CHAPTER 10

Benny Catches a Ghost

With one hand, Avery Drake shielded his eyes from the glare of Benny's flashlight.

"Benny!" he said, tightening his grip on the duffel bag with his other hand. "You're supposed to be in the soundstage with the others."

"And you're supposed to be in the control booth," Benny said. "But instead you're playing ghost."

At that moment, the overhead lights flickered back on. Grandfather, Jocelyn, and Earl rushed down the hall.

"Where is that tape playing from?" Jocelyn asked, as the screaming echoed throughout the station. "We've got to find it."

Gwen burst through the soundstage door.

"I know where it is!" she said. She dashed into the control booth. Jocelyn and Benny followed.

"What are you doing?" Avery asked, setting his duffel bag inside the cubby instead of its usual corner.

Gwen pushed aside Avery's box of half-eaten doughnuts, which was sitting on the console. A tiny cassette player, no bigger than a sandwich, was wedged between the box and the wall. Gwen hit the STOP button and the screaming ended. Now, only the voices of Henry, Violet, and Jessie came clearly over the speakers.

"Where did that come from?" Avery asked, sounding surprised.

"I've got to finish the show," Gwen said. "Don't let him leave!" She ran back to the soundstage.

Frances's voice told the listening audience she hoped they had enjoyed the program.

Gwen's music signaled the show was over.

"Excuse me," Avery said, reaching past Jocelyn to press buttons. "I have to cue up the commercial."

"Put on a prerecorded program next," Jocelyn told him. "We need to talk."

Avery searched through his CDs, then popped one into the CD player. An interview with a television star blasted through the speakers. Flipping a switch, Avery muted the sound in the studio.

When he looked up, Jessie, Henry, Benny, Violet, and Gwen were standing in the doorway, watching him.

"Well, Avery," Jocelyn began, "would you like to explain why you are 'haunting' the radio station?"

"That's ridiculous!" Avery said defensively. "I work here — why would I do anything to ruin my job?"

Frances leaned against the wall. "You tell us."

Avery crossed his arms and said nothing.

"When I saw you running last night," Gwen told Avery, "I remembered something." She walked over to the cubby and pushed back the curtain. Two empty hangers hung on the pole. The duffel bag sat on the floor.

"That's where you hang your clothes when you go running," Violet said. "You bring your running clothes and shoes in the duffel bag to the station every day."

"I change my clothes at the station after I run," Avery said. "What's so unusual about that?"

"When we saw you wearing your running clothes, you were also carrying the duffel bag," Henry said. "If your work clothes were here at the station, what were you carrying out of the station in the duffel bag?"

A short silence followed Henry's words.

"You use the duffel bag to take stuff *out* of the station," Benny concluded. "The stuff you were stealing."

Gwen spoke up. "And I bet it's also where you keep your ghostly sound effects tapes."

"You used the bag to smuggle out the microphone, which you took apart," Henry said to Avery. "The bag is big enough to hold that turntable, too. You put the turntable in the Dumpster outside, then went back later to get it."

"And you were in the station the other night to mess up Gwen's sound effects," Benny added. "We saw your flashlight through the windows. You switched the labels on her tapes. And yesterday, you stole Frances's script. That's what you were carrying in the duffel bag when we saw you running last night."

Avery was silent.

"Will you open your duffel bag?" Henry asked.

Avery hesitated, then retrieved his bag from the cubby. He unzipped it. Inside, under his running clothes, were several cassette tapes and the extra set of headphones.

Jessie stepped forward to read the labels on the cassettes. "SCREAMING. GHOSTLY MOANING. Pretty strange music."

Jocelyn took one of the tapes and popped it into the microcassette player. Loud moaning quavered through the speakers throughout the station. She pushed the

STOP button. Then she found a thin wire. "I suppose this goes to the speakers."

"Those are very good explanations," Avery said levelly. "But you've forgotten one thing — why would I do it? What's my motive?"

"To be a star," Violet said.

Avery laughed. "A star! Where did you get that crazy idea?"

"From the man you've been meeting in the Route 11 Diner," Jessie said. "He promised to make you a star DJ if you forced Jocelyn to sell the station. He wants to buy it."

Now Avery didn't look so confident. His shoulders sagged with defeat.

"Is this true?" Jocelyn demanded.

"Yes," he confessed. "The kids are right. A representative from MegaHits Corporation contacted me a few months ago. They still want to buy WCXZ."

"And turn it into an all-hits, all-the-time station?" Jocelyn guessed.

Avery nodded. "This guy wasn't the same man who tried to buy the station from

Luther. But it's the same company. If I helped them, they promised me a DJ job at their big station in the city. Do you know how many people would hear me then? Millions!"

"A lot more than in Deer Crossing," Jocelyn said wryly. "So you sold out. But why did you have to steal from me?"

"Because you wouldn't give up the station, Gran," Gwen explained. "Avery's only hope was that, if you had to keep replacing expensive equipment, you'd eventually *have* to sell."

"But why pretend a ghost is doing it?" Frances asked. "Why not just come into the station and steal stuff at night?"

"I could have," Avery said. "But I always liked that old story about Daphne Owens. I decided to make it look like she had come back. I never realized the mystery program cast would get so spooked they'd quit! When that happened, I thought I might be close to my goal . . . until the Aldens stepped in."

"So you also never realized that the real

Daphne Owens was a member of the cast," Henry said.

"What?" Avery looked shocked. So did Frances and Jocelyn.

"Daphne Owens got married and became DeeDee Rhoads," Violet explained. "She moved back to Deer Crossing, but kept her old identity a secret."

"I can't believe it!" Jocelyn said. "DeeDee is Daphne Owens!"

"DeeDee helped us," Jessie added. "She told us about the man that Avery met in the diner."

"You're not going to sell the station, are you, Gran?" Gwen asked.

"Of course not." Jocelyn turned to Avery. "You're fired. I ought to press charges, but I won't because Luther liked you. Pay me back for the equipment you stole and get out."

"I'm sorry," said Avery. "You and Luther have been so nice to me. But I got carried away with my dream. I'll be out by the end of the day. But who will run the station?"

"I will," said Jocelyn. "I'll be the DJ. I'm

going to add some programs. Gwen will help me."

"I'd like to sponsor the morning show, too," Earl offered. "If that's okay."

"Of course you can help, Earl. What about you?" Jocelyn asked Frances. "Are you staying with us?"

Frances shook her head. "Now that I have a really great script idea, I think it's time for me to start my movie-writing career. Plus, I really like writing for kids. I'd like to write a kids' movie, too. But I'm sure DeeDee Rhoads will jump at the chance to be the writer. She'll bring the cast back, too."

Jocelyn smiled at the Aldens. "Your grandfather was right. You are great detectives!"

Jessie smiled. "We couldn't have done it without Gwen!"

"I liked being a detective for a little while," said Gwen, "but I like working in Gran's station even better. I want to be a DJ."

"If you change your mind, you can join us," said Benny. "We'll be detectives forever!"